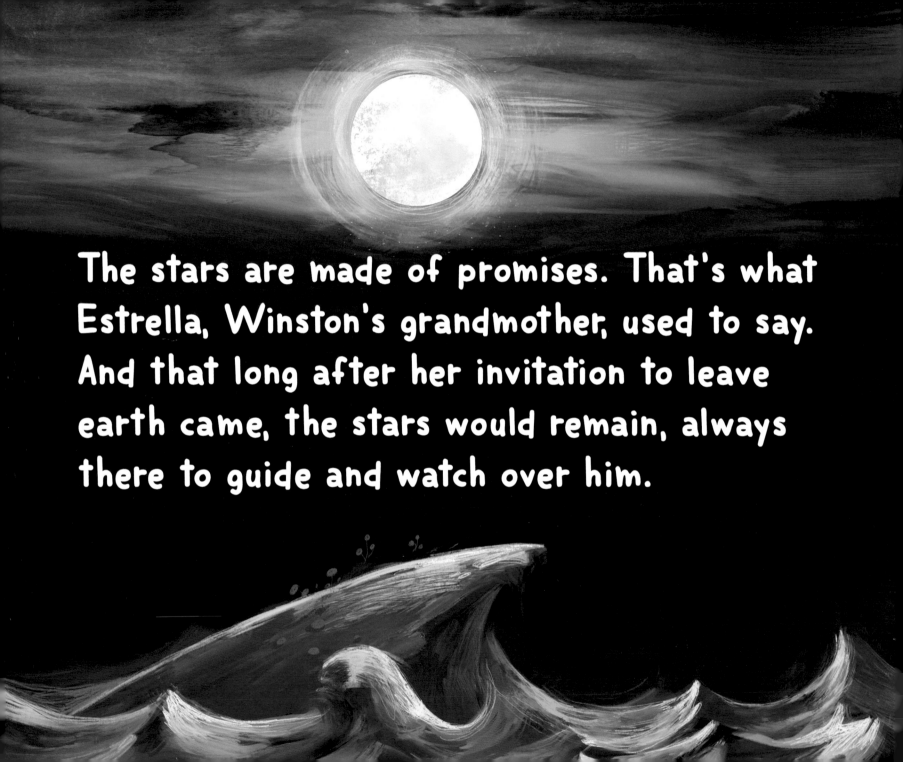

The stars are made of promises. That's what Estrella, Winston's grandmother, used to say. And that long after her invitation to leave earth came, the stars would remain, always there to guide and watch over him.

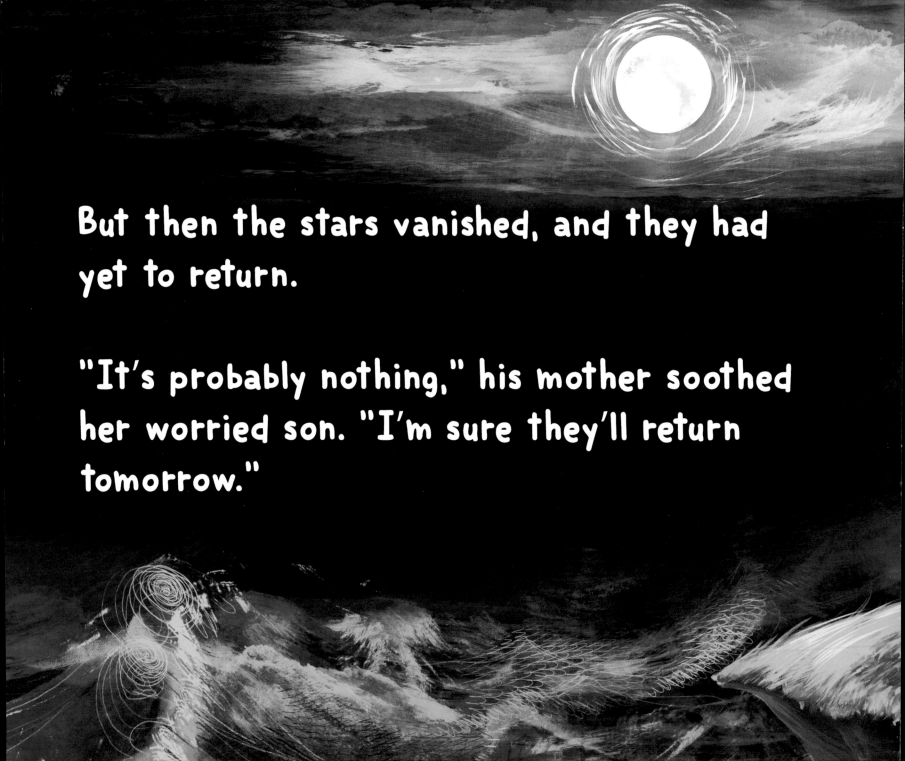

But then the stars vanished, and they had yet to return.

"It's probably nothing," his mother soothed her worried son. "I'm sure they'll return tomorrow."

"Where have you gone?" Winston asked, stealing one last glance at the empty sky.

Sleep did not find Winston this night.

He couldn't shake the feeling that something was wrong. If the stars were made of promises, and promises were not meant to be broken, then why had the stars vanished?

Then an idea came to him.

He would use the lighthouse's telescope to uncover a hiding star. But, all he found was a very tired, sleeping moon.

"Maybe the moon can help!" he thought, shining the light onto the moon. "Hello, Moon!" Winston called out.

"I'm so sorry to wake you," Winston said. "But I need your help."

"Whatever would you need me for?" asked the Moon with a yawn.

"I can't find the stars," Winston admitted. "They seem to have gone missing."

"Oh, yes," said the Moon. "I am aware of this. They are hiding. And scared they are."

"Scared?" Winston repeated. "What could the stars be afraid of?"

"Why don't you come up and find out?" the Moon suggested.

"Me? Go up there? But I can't," Winston said. "I'm down here and, well, the stars are up there."

"Oh, I don't think that's a problem at all," said the Moon.

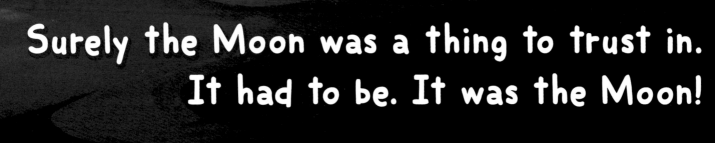

Surely the Moon was a thing to trust in.
It had to be. It was the Moon!

Before he knew it, he was in the clouds. Walking on them!

But then something else caught his attention. A glowing object that zig-zagged through the fluffy clouds like a dolphin in the ocean.

The mysterious shape suddenly fell over and let out a loud groan. "Hellooooo?" Its voice followed.

Winston looked around but found no one. "Hello?" he answered back.

"Oh! Someone is there!" the voice cried out. "Will you help me, please?"

Plopped on its back
was a plump, big-eyed star!

"Thank you," said the shooting star.
"Sometimes I go too fast and
fall over." He chuckled.
"Last time I was down for weeks."

"I'm sorry about that," said Winston.
"Oh! Maybe you can help me.
I'm looking for the other stars.
Do you know where they've gone?"

"Oh, yes," said the star. "Of course I do. Why wouldn't I know where they are? Do you know where the stars are?"

"No," admitted Winston. "Will ... you help me find them?"

"Well," considered the star, "You did help me. And it does get quite boring. I suppose I can help."

"Thank you!" jeered Winston. "The Moon told me they were hiding. But why?"

"The question is, why wouldn't we be?" the star said.

"So many broken promises. From up here we see everything. Look what's happened to our friend, the Earth. The humans have put so much stress on her."

"You can barely see the skies through all the pollution. The oceans are littered with waste. There are even islands made up of all the trash." Star shook his head and throbbed with light. "The humans promised to take care of the earth. How are we not to think that we are next?"

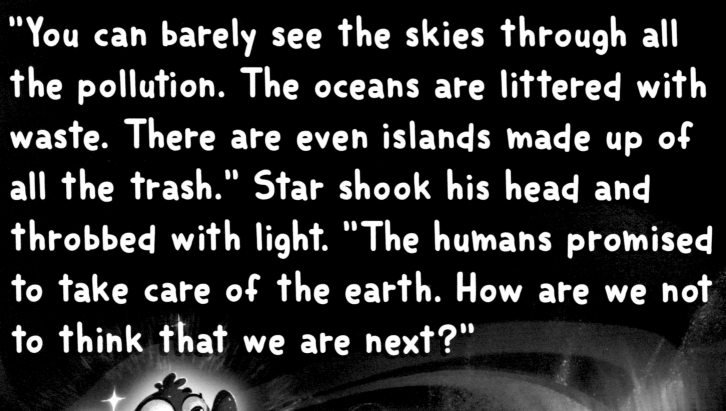
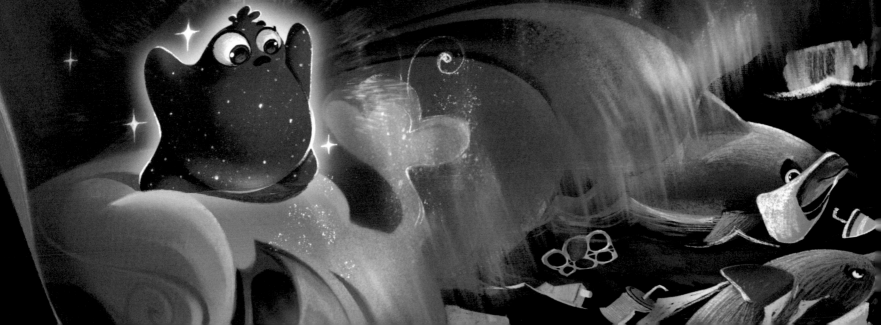

Winston felt the pain of the stars in his chest. Of course they were afraid.

"There's no time to cry," said the shooting star. "It's time to act. To make a change."

"But what can I do?" Winston asked. "I'm just a boy."

"That's where you are wrong," said Star. "You are a boy in the clouds."

Star was right. It was time to act!

"Lead the way," Winston said, buzzing with pride and excitement.

"Follow me!" Star exclaimed. Then he paused and said, "Actually, would you mind giving me a lift? I'm pooped."

The path to the stars led them through a magical forest, with rivers made of rainbows and dancing space plants.

"That's the entrance," said Star.
"I'll need your help to open it."

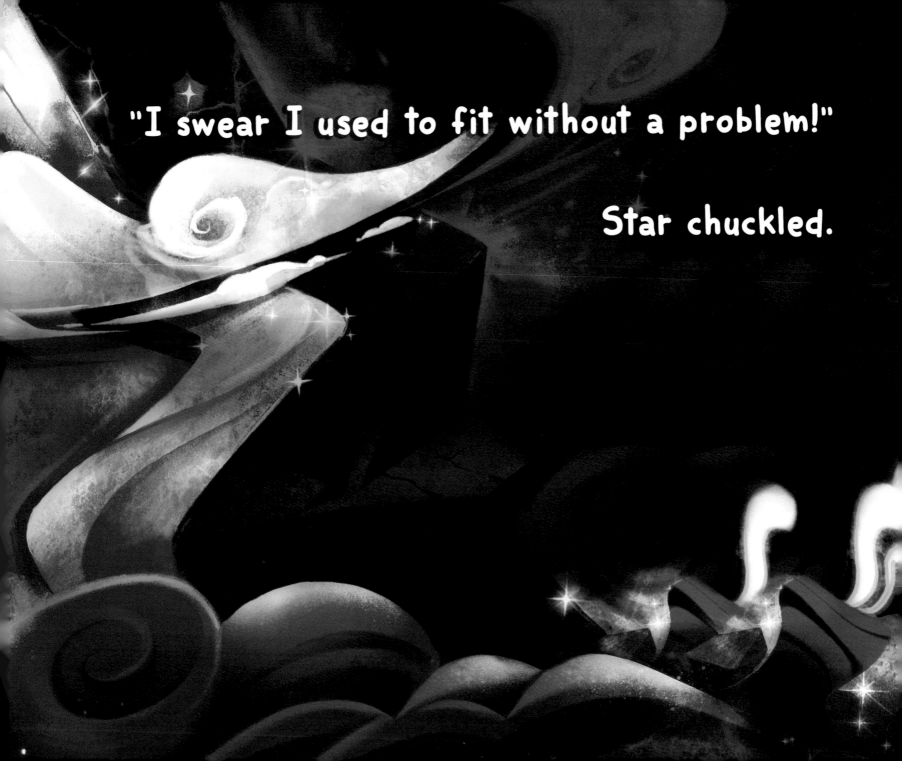

"I swear I used to fit without a problem!"

Star chuckled.

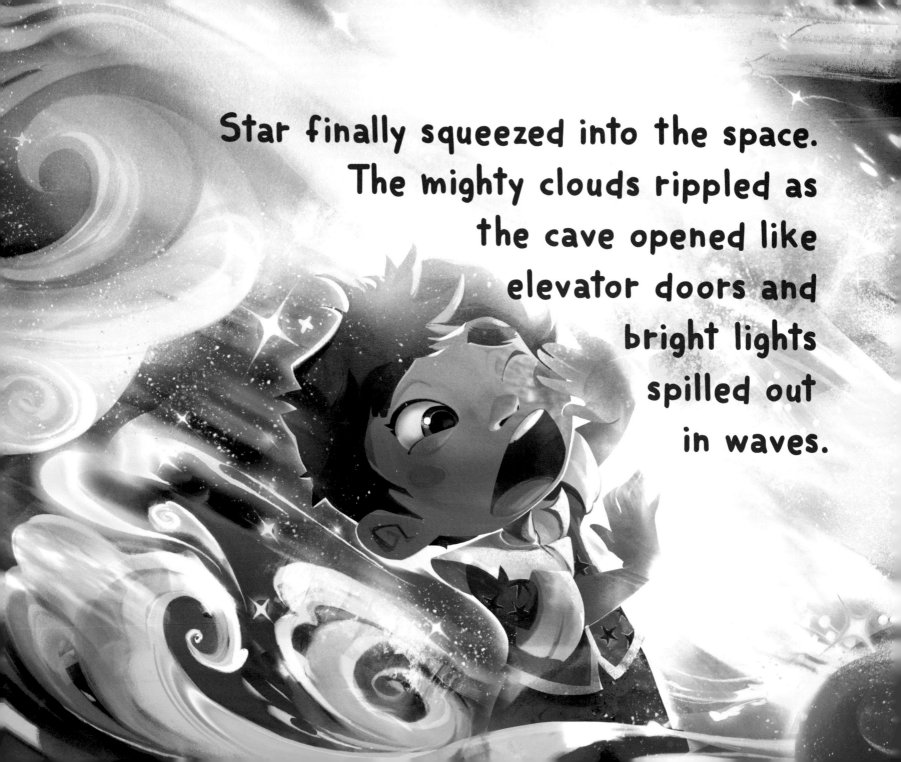

Star finally squeezed into the space. The mighty clouds rippled as the cave opened like elevator doors and bright lights spilled out in waves.

Then... there they were.

The stars.

An entire village of them.

Everything fell silent and
all eyes locked on Winston.

Then a star dropped her bag
and shouted. "HUMAN!"

Within seconds there were
only streaks of colored light.

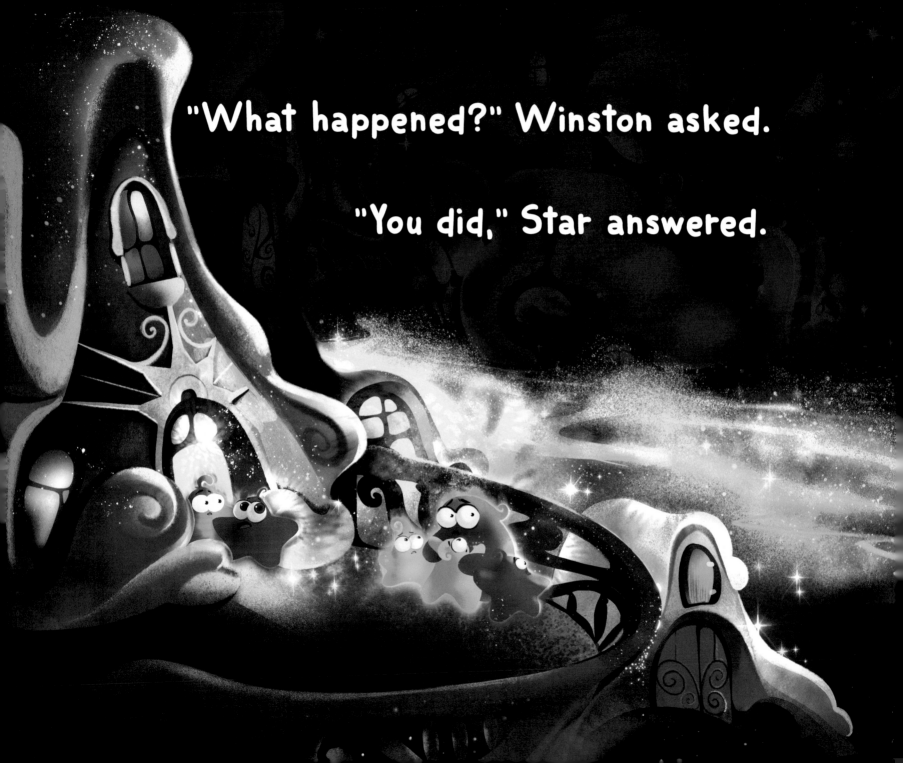

A tiny star trembled behind a bin.

"I'm not here to hurt you,"

Winston said in a soft voice.

"I'm your friend."

"Why would we trust you?"
A fiery red star shouted.
"Look at what's happened to Earth!
How do you explain that?"

"I don't know," Winston admitted. "But I promise that there are more like me. So many who care, and love the planet and the stars."

"And why should we believe YOU ?" asked another star.

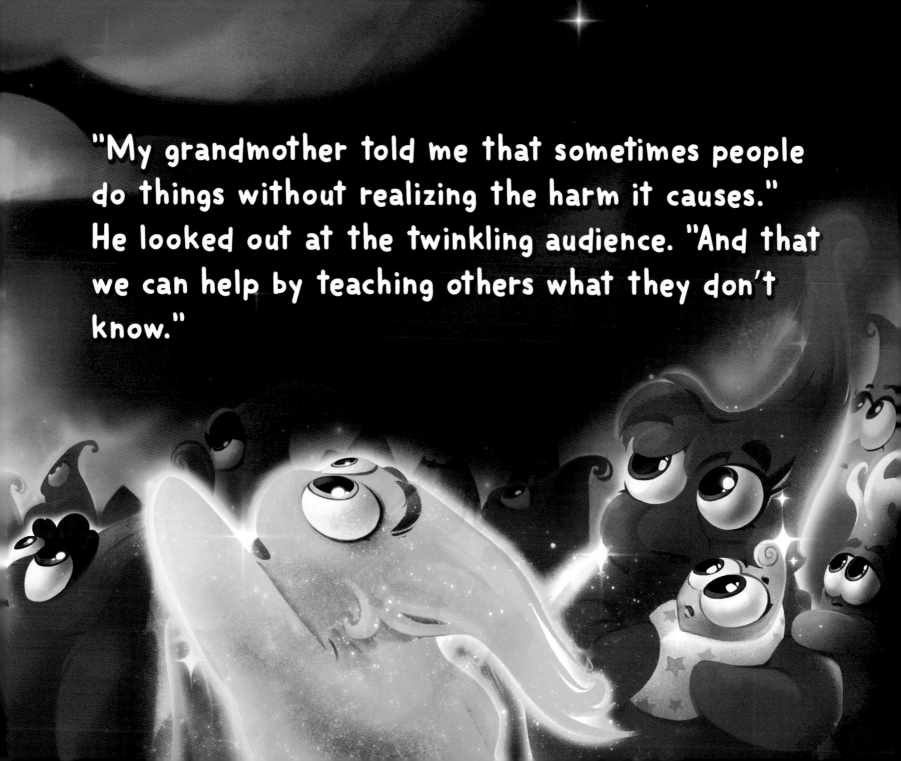

"My grandmother told me that sometimes people do things without realizing the harm it causes." He looked out at the twinkling audience. "And that we can help by teaching others what they don't know."

"He's right!" shouted the shooting star.

"We can't give up on them. We all share this space. If you think about it... we all have the same to lose."

"I know you don't have a reason to trust me, so take this," Winston said, grabbing his necklace. "My grandmother gave it to me before she left us. Nothing I have means more to me."

A loud gasp rippled over the stars.

"You would give up something so important to you?" asked the red star.

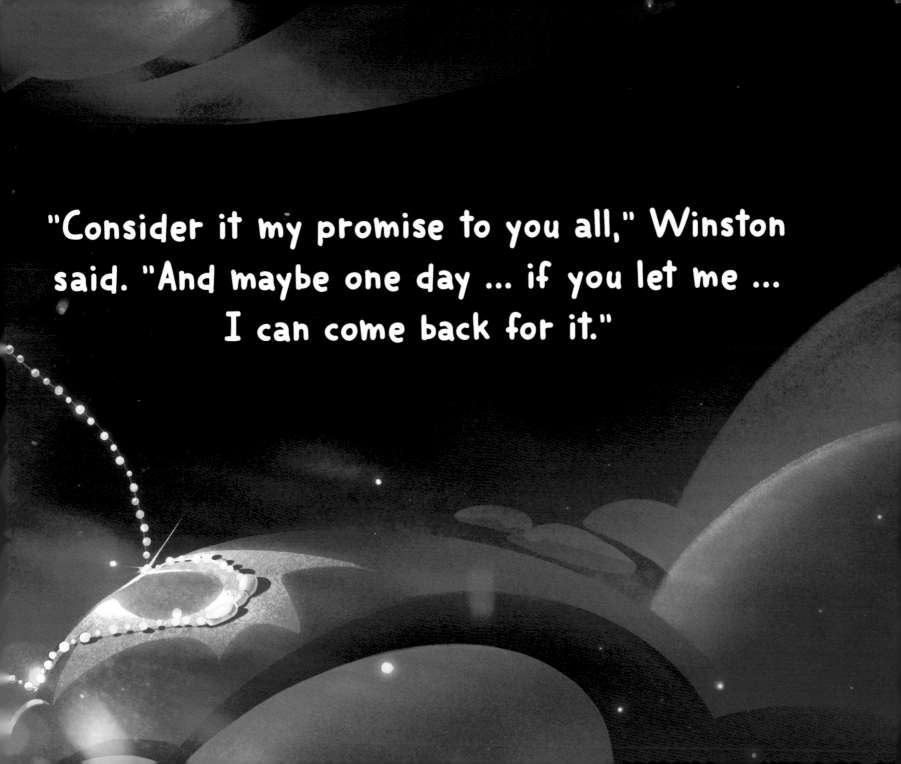

"Consider it my promise to you all," Winston said. "And maybe one day ... if you let me ... I can come back for it."

"We will care for it like it is our very own," promised the red star, admiring the necklace.

"And I'll do the same with our planet," Winston said.

"And there are more like you?"
asked a star.

"Millions,"
replied Winston.

"Then, we shall decide tonight,"
said the red star.
"For now, sleep, Winston."

Winston woke up in his room, but it was now morning. He panicked, thinking it had all been a dream until the sun hit his arm and a streak of stardust sparkled.
It was real!

That meant there was no time to waste!
Winston jumped right into action.

Later that night, his mother called him to the window.

He looked up at the sky, filled with more stars than he had ever seen.

His grandmother had said the stars were made of promises. And tonight, he felt the truth of it in his heart. Each star was a promise he had made, a sky worth of vows he would never break.

And as he watched the stars twinkle on this particular night, Winston felt closer to his grandmother, Estrella,
than he ever had.

Winston would share
the story of when the stars went missing,
and of the day he guided them back home.

He would point up to the sky and remind
others that promises were more than
words. That unbroken promises lit up
our skies and guided our paths
into the unknown.

Hardcover: 978-0-9888916-9-2
Ebook: 979-8-9886349-0-4

Illustrations by Krapivina Olga
Layout Design by Carlos Torrez

Hello, Wonderworld
www.hellowonderworld.com

www.thenightthestarswentmissing.com